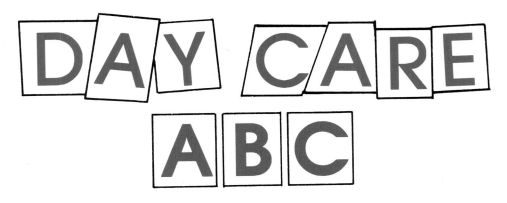

# DAY CARE ABC

**TAMARA PHILLIPS**     *pictures by DORA LEDER*

Albert Whitman & Company, Niles, Illinois

*For my children. **T.P.***
*For Jill, Phil, and Hannah Leigh. **D.L.***

*Text © 1989 by Tamara Phillips.*
*Illustrations © 1989 by Dora Leder.*
*Design by Karen A. Yops.*

Published in 1989 by Albert Whitman & Company,
5747 West Howard Street, Niles, Illinois 60648.
Published simultaneously in Canada
by General Publishing, Limited, Toronto.
All rights reserved.
Printed in the United States of America.
10 9 8 7 6 5 4 3 2 1

Library of Congress Cataloging-in-Publication Data

Phillips, Tamara.
Day care ABC.
Summary: Twenty-six children perform day care center
activities that match their names alphabetically, from
Adam asking for applesauce to Zoe zipping her zipper.
[1. Day care centers—Fiction.   2. Alphabet]
I. Leder, Dora, ill.   II. Title.
PZ7.P5465Day   1989   [E]   88-33911
ISBN 0-8075-1483-7

Adam asks for applesauce.

Brenda brushes her bangs.

Corey carries his crocodile.

Daniel's dad drives him to day care.

Ms. Edwards enjoys greeting everyone.

Franky finds his friends.

Gloria gets the glue.

Heather helps cut hearts.

Irene is interested in insects.

Joshua joins the job.

Kimberly knows the way to the kitchen.

Luis likes lemonade.

Meryl munches macaroni.

Mr. Nash notes it's naptime.

Oliver owns an orange blanket.

Paula pats her panda.

Quentin quietly folds his quilt.

Rosalba runs to see the rabbit.

Sam shares a swing.

Talia turns the tricycle.

Umeko unfolds the umbrella.

Vincent volunteers to vacuum.

William washes the window.

Xavier examines the xylophone.

Yolanda yells, "Yippee! Mommy's here!"

Zoe zips her zipper.

*Here are some objects and colors you can see*
*in the pictures. Can you find more?*

**A**corns
airplane
animals
anteater
apples
applesauce
apple tree
apron
argyle vest
artichoke
artwork

**B**all
balloons
bandanna
bangs
banister
barrettes
bear
bed
belt
birds
blanket
blue
book
boot
bowl
box
braids
bristles
brown
brush
buckle
bunnies
bureau
butterflies
button

**C**alico cat
camera
car
cherries
chimney
circles
city
clouds
collar
corduroy
country
cows
crayons
crocodile
curls

**D**ad
daisy
Dalmatian
diaper
dinosaur
dog
doll
dominoes
door
dots
drapes
drums
ducks

**E**agle
earmuffs
earrings
Easter eggs
eight
elephant
Eskimo
eyeglasses

**F**eather
fern
fire truck
fish
fish food
five
floor
flowers
football
frog

**G**iraffe
girl
glasses
globe
glue
gold
goose
grapes
grass
gray
green

**H**air
hat
hatband
headband
hearts
helicopter
hexagon
hippo
horn
house

**I**ce
ice cream cones
igloo
ink
insects
iron
ivy

**J**acket
jack-in-the-box
jacks
jaguar
jar
jeans
jeep
jet
jump rope

**K**angaroos
kerchief
kettle
keys
kids
kilt
kiss
kitchen
kite
kiwis
knives
koala

**Lace**
lap
lavender
leaves
lemonade
lettuce
locket
lunch
lunchbox

**Macaroni**
milk
monkey
moon
mountains
mouse
mug
mushrooms

**Necklace**
necktie
nest
nines
numbers
nurse

**Octopus**
orange
overalls
owl

**Panda**
pants
paper
parrot
paws
pencils
penguins
pillow
pink
plaid
polka dots
purple

**Queen**
quilt
question marks

**Rabbit**
racket
rainbow
rake
red
redhead
ribbon
ring
roofs
rose
ruby

**Sand**
sandals
sevens
shoes
sieve
silver
sixes
sneakers
socks
stars
stripes
swing
sun

**Tail**
tambourine
ten
tires
toys
train
tree
tricycle
truck
T-shirt
turtle
twins
two

**Ukulele**
umbrellas
unicorn
uniform
upside-down bear

**Vacuum cleaner**
valentines
vegetables
vests
violet
violin
v-neck sweater

**Wagon**
walrus
washcloth
watch
water
wet spots
wheels
white
window
windowsill
witch

**Xylophone**

**Yardstick**
yarn
yawn
yellow
yo-yo

**Zebra**
zigzags
zippers
zoo

## ABOUT THE AUTHOR

TAMARA PHILLIPS lives near San Francisco with her husband, Vincent, and their two young children, Adam and Meryl, both of whom attended day care programs. Tamara says she has read hundreds of stories to her children; she wrote DAY CARE ABC so they could read a book their mother had written.

## ABOUT THE ARTIST

DORA LEDER lives in rural Bucks County, Pennsylvania, with her husband, Ed, five cats, one large dog, and a hamster. She has illustrated more than forty books for children as well as numerous textbook and magazine stories. DAY CARE ABC is her thirteenth book for Albert Whitman.